CARTER HIGH
SENIOR YEAR

IT DOES
Matter

By Eleanor Robins

SADDLEBACK
EDUCATIONAL PUBLISHING

CARTER HIGH
SENIOR YEAR

SADDLEBACK
EDUCATIONAL PUBLISHING
www.sdlback.com

ISBN-13: 978-1-61651-324-5
ISBN-10: 1-61651-324-1
eBook: 978-1-60291-972-3

Printed in Guangzhou, China
0910/09-42-10

15 14 13 12 11   1 2 3 4 5

Chapter 1

Laine walked to school. Tess was with her. Tess was Laine's best friend. And Tess was in her English class.

Tess didn't share any other classes with Laine. But they did have lunch at the same time.

Tess was in a hurry to get to school. But Laine wasn't in a hurry.

Laine liked school OK. But she was very glad it was her senior year. School would be over in three weeks. Laine could hardly wait.

Tess asked, "Why did you get to my house so late? I told you I wanted to get to school early."

Laine was in a hurry for her senior year to be over. But that didn't mean she wanted to get to school early.

"I don't know why you are so upset, Tess. I got to your house late. So what? It doesn't matter. We will still get to school on time," Laine said.

Tess said, "But it does matter to me. I need to talk to Mrs. Vance before school starts. I need to ask her about our test."

Mrs. Vance was their English teacher. They had a test in her class the next day. It would be the last test before their final exam.

"Mrs. Vance is going to review the test for us today. So ask her then," Laine said.

"I need to ask her now. I might not get a chance to ask her in class. It will be a hard test. And I want to do well on it," Tess said.

Tess always studied a lot. And she worried a lot about her grades.

Laine thought Tess worried too much about her grades.

Laine said, "Don't worry about the test, Tess. I am sure you will do well on it. We are almost to school. So you can talk to Mrs. Vance before school starts."

"But I have a book due today. I need to take it back to the media center. I want to take it back before school starts. And now I can't do that," Tess said.

"You can take it back after lunch," Laine said.

Tess said, "I know. But I don't want to do that. And now I will have to take it then. You should have been on time, Laine."

Laine didn't know why Tess was so upset. Tess had time to talk to Mrs. Vance before school started. And it didn't

matter about her book. Tess could take it back after lunch.

Laine wanted them to talk about something else. She tried to think of something to say. Then she thought about the game on Friday after school.

The Carter High baseball team was going to play Maxwell High. The game would be played at Maxwell High. The winner would go to the state finals.

Laine was going to the game. She would ride the school bus. Griff was going on the bus too.

Griff was her boyfriend. They had been dating for most of the school year.

Laine said, "I wish you could go to the game on Friday."

Tess said, "So do I. I wish it were here. Then I could go. But I can't go to Maxwell High. I would get home too late.

"My cousins are coming to visit. They

might already be at my house. And I have to be home when they get there."

Her two cousins were coming from out of town. Her aunt and uncle were coming too. They were going to stay all weekend.

The girls got to the school.

Tess said, "I need to hurry. I will see you in English class."

Tess hurried in the school.

Laine walked around outside for a few minutes. She saw Steve.

Steve was in her English class too. He and Griff were friends. Steve always studied a lot. But Laine thought he worried too much about his grades too.

Laine was looking for Griff. But she didn't see him.

The bell rang.

Laine went in the school. She walked

slowly to her first class. Griff wasn't in her first class. So she was in no hurry to get there.

Laine was almost late to class.

Chapter 2

Laine was glad her first class was over.

Laine had Mrs. Vance next. Mrs. Vance was going to review their test. So Laine knew she needed to hurry to class.

Laine saw Griff. He was in the hall.

Griff was talking to Marge. Marge had been in a class with Laine last year.

Marge went in a classroom. Griff went on down the hall. Laine hurried after him.

Laine said, "Wait, Griff. I want to talk to you."

Griff stopped. He was almost to his class.

Laine hurried up to him.

Griff said, "I don't have time to talk. I have to get to class. I don't want to be late. And you have to get to class too."

Laine knew she should hurry to class. But she had to talk to Griff first.

Laine asked, "Why were you talking to Marge?"

"She asked me how to do our homework," Griff said.

"Why would Marge ask you about homework?" Laine asked.

Griff said, "I study now. And Marge thought I would know how to do it."

Laine found out what she wanted to know.

So she said, "I will see you in science class after lunch."

Then Laine went on down the hall.

Griff would be on time to class. But Laine would be late. And she would get into trouble.

Laine saw Mrs. Dodd. Mrs. Dodd was her history teacher.

It was Mrs. Dodd's planning time. She was pushing a cart. It had a lot of books on it.

Laine hurried over to her. Maybe she could help Mrs. Dodd. Then Mrs. Dodd would give her a late pass.

Laine could be late. It would be OK. She wouldn't get into trouble.

"Do you need some help, Mrs. Dodd?" Laine asked.

"Yes, Laine. But you don't have time to help me. You need to get to class. You will be late," Mrs. Dodd said.

Laine said, "That is OK. I can be late. Will you give me a late pass?"

Laine helped Mrs. Dodd. Then Mrs. Dodd gave her a late pass.

Laine hurried to class. She was very

late. But she knew she would be. She had missed some of the review.

Laine hurried in her classroom.

Mrs. Vance asked, "Why are you late, Laine? Do you have a late pass?"

"Yes," Laine said.

She quickly gave her late pass to Mrs. Vance. Then she sat down next to Tess.

Mrs. Vance looked at her late pass.

Then Mrs. Vance told the class some more about their test.

It was almost time for class to be over.

Mrs. Vance said, "I hope you know what to study. Does anyone have a question?"

"I do," Laine said. Laine asked her question.

Then Mrs. Vance said, "I went over that before you came. But I will go over it again for you, Laine."

Then Laine asked two more questions. And Mrs. Vance told Laine the answer to each of them.

Steve said, "I need to ask you something, Mrs. Vance."

The bell rang.

Mrs. Vance said, "I am sorry, Steve. Class is over. I don't have time to answer any more questions."

Laine was glad the class was over. She started to walk out the door with Tess.

Tess asked, "Why were you late?"

Laine said, "Griff was talking to Marge. I had to find out why. So I stopped to talk to him. I knew I would be late. Then I helped Mrs. Dodd so I could get a late pass."

"You should have talked to Griff later. You knew we were going to review the test. You should have gotten to class on time," Tess said.

"So what? It doesn't matter. Mrs.

Vance told me what I needed to know," Laine said.

"I know she did. But she had already told the rest of the class. So you wasted our class time. That wasn't fair to us," Tess said.

"You are the only one who feels that way. The rest of the class didn't care," Laine said.

"You are wrong. They did care. No one likes it when someone else wastes the class time. And we didn't have time for Steve to ask his question," Tess said.

Laine didn't know why Tess was so upset with her. She was late. So what? It didn't matter.

Chapter 3

It was Friday. The Maxwell High game was today.

The end of school bell rang. Laine got up and left her class. But she didn't hurry. She went to her locker.

Laine saw Tess. Tess was at her locker too.

Tess asked, "Are you still going to the game?"

"Yes. Why?" Laine asked.

"I thought you were going on the bus," Tess said.

"I am," Laine said.

"Then you need to hurry, Laine. You

know Griff likes to be the first one on the bus. Then he can get the seat he wants. You need to get there before he gets on the bus. That way you can sit with him," Tess said.

"I can be a few minutes late. It doesn't matter. Griff knows I am going on the bus. He will wait for me," Laine said.

"Don't be too sure about that, Laine. You know how he is," Tess said.

Laine knew Griff wanted to sit with her. And she was sure he would wait for her. So Laine didn't hurry.

Laine got to the bus. Griff wasn't waiting outside the bus for her.

Laine looked at the students on the bus.

She saw Griff. He was sitting with Marge. Marge had a big smile on her face.

How could Griff get on the bus before she got there? And why didn't he save her a seat?

Laine got on the bus. She had to walk by Griff and Marge.

Marge said, "Hi, Laine."

Griff didn't say anything to Laine. And Laine didn't say anything to him. She didn't speak to Marge either.

Laine hurried past them. She sat down in a seat.

The bus trip wasn't that long. But it seemed long to Laine. She was glad when they got to Maxwell High.

Griff quickly got up. He got off the bus.

Laine got off the bus too. She hurried over to Griff.

She said, "I saw you."

And she didn't say it in a nice way.

"So? I saw you too," Griff said.

"Why did you sit with Marge?" Laine asked.

And she didn't ask that in a nice way.

"I didn't sit with Marge. She sat with

me," Griff said.

"It's the same thing," Laine said.

Griff said, "No, it isn't. I sat on the bus. Then Marge got on the bus. She sat down next to me."

"You didn't have to let her sit there. And you should have told her not to sit there," Laine said.

"Why? She had to sit somewhere. And you were late. So I don't know why you are mad. It isn't my fault Marge sat with me. It's your fault," Griff said.

"And just how is it my fault?" Laine asked.

"You were late," Griff said.

"So what? It doesn't matter. You knew I was going to ride the bus. And you knew I wanted to sit with you. So you should have saved me a seat," Laine said.

"No. You should have been on time," Griff said.

"No. You should have saved me a seat. So forget about our date tomorrow night," Laine said.

"Fine," Griff said.

Then he walked off.

Laine didn't care. She didn't know why he was mad. It was all his fault. It wasn't her fault at all.

Laine went to the stands to get a seat. She saw Griff. He looked over at her.

She wanted to sit with him. But he didn't ask her to sit with him. So she sat with some other students.

Laine wanted to sit with Griff on the bus ride back to Carter High too.

But Griff didn't ask Laine to sit with him. Laine sat by herself.

Chapter 4

It was the next morning. Laine was at home. She was in her room. Her room was a mess.

Laine was getting ready to go outside. She wanted to shoot some baskets.

Her mom came in her room.

"You have to clean your room, Laine. I told you all week to clean it. And you said you would do it later. So you have to clean your room this morning. Don't forget to do it," her mom said.

"OK," Laine said.

Then her mom left.

Laine knew she should clean her

room. But she didn't want to do it now. She wanted to go outside. And she wanted to shoot some baskets.

She didn't have any plans with Griff now. And Tess had to stay home with her cousins. So Laine had all day to clean her room. She would shoot baskets now. And then she would clean her room after lunch.

Laine started to go outside.

The phone rang.

It was Tess.

Tess said, "My cousins didn't come after all."

Laine wanted to talk to Tess about Griff. So she was glad Tess called.

"What are you doing this morning?" Tess asked.

"I am getting ready to shoot some baskets," Laine said.

"Why? Basketball season is over,"

Tess said.

"I know. But I'd still like to shoot some baskets," Laine said.

Laine and Tess had both been on the starting basketball team. Laine was the high scorer.

"Are you doing something with Griff today?" Tess asked.

Laine told her about the trip to Maxwell High. And she told Tess about her fight with Griff.

Tess said, "That is too bad. Maybe he will call you today."

"Maybe," Laine said.

She hoped he would call. But she wasn't sure he would.

"What are you going to do after lunch?" Tess asked.

"I will clean my room. Mom said I had to do it today. Why?" Laine asked.

"I thought you might want to do

something with me. But you need to clean your room," Tess said.

"That is OK. I can do it next week," Laine said.

"I thought you had to do it today," Tess said.

"No. I can do it next week. Mom won't care," Laine said.

"Are you sure she won't care?" Tess asked.

"Yes. What do you want to do?" Laine asked.

"I want to go to a movie. Is that OK with you?" Tess asked.

"Which movie?" Laine asked.

Tess told her.

"OK. When does the movie start?" Laine asked.

Tess said, "It starts at 2:15. Can you meet me outside the theater at 2:00?"

"OK," Laine said.

"You know I always like to be on time to a movie. So don't be late," Tess said.

"I won't be," Laine said.

Tess hung up.

Laine started to go outside.

Her mom asked, "Where are you going, Laine?"

"I'm going outside. I want to shoot some baskets," Laine said.

"You will have to do that later, Laine. Right now you need to clean your room," her mom said.

"I can do that later, Mom," Laine said.

"No, Laine. You can't play now. You told me all week that you would clean up later. But you didn't. So that later is now. Get busy cleaning," her mom said.

Laine cleaned her room. She had a lot to do. So it took her a long time.

Then Laine went outside to shoot some baskets.

Laine was having fun. She forgot about meeting Tess later that day. And she also forgot to keep up with the time

She didn't get to the movie until 2:15

Tess was waiting outside for her. Tess looked upset.

"Why are you late, Laine? You know the movie starts at 2:15," Tess said.

"I was shooting some baskets. I forgot about the time," Laine said.

"Now we will be late," Tess said.

"So what? It doesn't matter. The movie has just started. We are only a few minutes late. You won't miss much," Laine said.

"It does matter to me. I don't like to see a movie after it starts. And you know that," Tess said.

Laine didn't know why Tess was upset. Tess would miss only a few minutes of the movie.

Chapter 5

It was Monday. Laine was on her way to lunch. She looked for Griff. She hadn't seen him all morning. And he didn't call her over the weekend.

Then Laine saw Griff. He walked down the hall. He looked at her. But he didn't speak to her. And there was no way Laine would speak to him first.

Laine went on to lunch.

Tess was waiting for Laine at the lunchroom door. The girls went inside. They got their trays. Then they went to a table and sat down.

Tess asked, "Have you seen Griff today?"

"Yes. I saw him in the hall. I was on my way to lunch," Laine said.

"Did he talk to you?" Tess asked.

"No," Laine said.

"Too bad. Did you talk to him?" Tess asked.

"No," Laine said.

"Why didn't you?" Tess asked.

"He didn't talk to me first," Laine said.

"That is silly, Laine. You should have talked to him," Tess said.

"He should have called me. But he didn't call," Laine said.

"Maybe you should have called him," Tess said.

Laine said, "No way. I am waiting for him to tell me he is sorry."

"What is he sorry about?" Tess asked.

Laine said, "You know what. He didn't save me a seat on Friday. And he knew I wanted to sit with him."

"But you were late," Tess said.

"So what? It doesn't matter. He still should have saved me a seat," Laine said.

"Do you still like him?" Tess asked.

Laine wanted to say no. But that wasn't true. And she knew Tess wouldn't believe her.

"Yes," Laine said.

"Then be nice to him. And don't act as if you are mad at him," Tess said.

"But I am mad at him," Laine said.

"I know you are. But you don't have to let Griff know that. So speak to him the next time you see him. Then maybe he will talk to you," Tess said.

"No way. He will have to talk to me first," Laine said.

"Don't wait for Griff to talk to you first. You know how Griff is, Laine. He might never do that," Tess said.

Laine knew Tess was right about Griff.

The girls needed to eat. So they stopped talking. They ate their lunch. Then it was time for them to go to class.

Tess said, "Don't forget what I said, Laine. Speak to Griff the next time you see him."

"I will think about it," Laine said.

She would think about it. But she wasn't sure she would speak to Griff first.

Chapter 6

Laine didn't see Griff until she went to science class. Griff was already there.

Laine went to her desk and sat down. She sat next to Griff. Griff looked at her. But he didn't speak to her. And Laine didn't speak to him.

The bell rang. Mr. Reese started the class.

Laine couldn't keep her mind on the class. She kept looking at Griff. And he kept looking at her.

Laine thought about what Tess had said to her. She did like Griff. Maybe she should speak to him first. But she still hoped he would speak to her first.

Laine was glad when the class was over. She hoped Griff would say something to her. But Griff didn't speak to her. He got up from his desk. And then he quickly left the class.

Laine hurried after him.

She said, "Wait, Griff."

Griff stopped. But he didn't turn around.

Laine hurried up to him.

Laine said, "You should have called me."

Griff asked, "Why? I knew you wouldn't talk to me. So why should I have called?"

"Maybe I would have talked to you. You should have called me to find out," Laine said.

"Would you have talked to me?" Griff asked.

"No. But you still should have called me," Laine said.

"Why?" Griff asked.

"So I could tell you I wouldn't talk to you," Laine said.

"Then it is good I didn't call you. But you should have called me," Griff said.

"Why? It was your fault," Laine said.

"It wasn't my fault," Griff said.

Laine wanted to tell him again that it was his fault. But she didn't say any more.

She said, "Maybe some of it was my fault."

Griff seemed surprised she said that.

He said, "Maybe I should have called you."

That surprised Laine.

"Maybe I should have called you," Laine said.

Carter High would play in the state finals Saturday. Laine was going to the game. She would ride the school bus.

She thought Griff was going to the game too. But she wasn't sure about that.

Laine said, "I am going to the ballgame on Saturday. Are you going?"

"Yeah," Griff said.

"Are you going on the bus?" Laine asked.

"Yeah," Griff said.

"Will you save me a seat?" Laine asked.

"The bus leaves at 8:30," Griff said.

"I know," Laine said.

"Can you be there by 8:10?" Griff asked.

"Yes," Laine said.

"Then I will save you a seat. But be at the bus by 8:10. Or I will let someone else sit with me," Griff said.

Laine said, "OK. I will be there by 8:10."

"You had better be. Or I will let some-one else sit with me. And you had better not get mad about it," Griff said.

"OK. I won't get mad about it. But I will be there on time. I won't be late," Laine said.

Laine wanted to sit with Griff. So there was no way she would be late. She would be at the bus by 8:10.

Chapter 7

It was two days later. Laine was in her English class. Tess and Steve were there too.

Mrs. Vance said, "I graded your test papers. Some of you did very well. Some of you didn't."

It was a hard test. Laine hoped she did well on it. She studied a lot for it. So she thought she did well.

Mrs. Vance said, "Your final exam is next week."

All of Laine's exams were next week. She would finish high school in two weeks.

Laine could hardly wait for the school year to be over.

Mrs. Vance said, "We will review your exam tomorrow. Be sure you are all on time to class. Don't be late for any reason."

Mrs. Vance looked at Laine.

Then Mrs. Vance passed out the test papers.

Laine made a good grade. Mrs. Vance answered her questions on the review day. That was why she did well.

Mrs. Vance said, "All of you need to study for your exam. You need to make a good grade on it. You don't want to take this class again this summer. And you don't want to come back next year."

The bell rang.

Laine and Tess got their books. They quickly went out in the hall.

Steve was behind them.

Steve said, "Don't be late tomorrow,

Laine. Get here on time. I made a bad grade because of you."

And he didn't say that in a nice way.

"Don't blame me. You should have studied. I studied," Laine said.

Steve said, "I did study. But I needed to ask Mrs. Vance something. And you were late. So she spent time telling you what you missed. And that wasted our class time. So I didn't have time to ask Mrs. Vance my question."

Laine didn't know why Steve was so upset. He could have stayed after class. He could have asked Mrs. Vance then.

Mrs. Vance would have given him a late pass. Then he could have been late to his next class. And that would have been OK.

Laine said, "You could have stayed after class. And you could have asked Mrs. Vance then."

"No. I couldn't have. I had to get to my next class on time. I couldn't be late to it," Steve said.

Laine said, "Yes, you could have been late. Mrs. Vance would have given you a late pass."

Steve said, "But I didn't want to be late to it. I try to get to class on time. I want to be fair to the other students in my class. I don't want to waste their time."

Laine got to her next class. She didn't want to talk to Steve anymore. And she was glad he wasn't in this class.

Laine hurried in her classroom.

Steve called after her.

He said, "Be on time tomorrow, Laine."

Then he went on down the hall.

Chapter 8

It was Saturday. Laine was on her way to see Tess. Tess was going to the ballgame too.

Laine was in a hurry to get to her house. Laine wanted to get to the bus on time. That way she could sit with Griff.

Laine got to Tess's house. Tess said she would meet Laine in front of her house. But Laine didn't see Tess at all.

Laine was sure Tess would be right out. But then Tess didn't come right out.

Laine waited for a few minutes. Then she hurried to the door. She rang the bell.

Tess opened the door. Then she quickly hurried outside.

Laine said, "We are going to be late. Don't you know what time it is?"

"Yes," Tess said.

Laine had wanted to get to the bus on time. It meant a lot to her. And Tess knew that it did.

"You knew I wanted to get to school by 8:10. Why weren't you waiting for me outside? You said you would be," Laine said.

Tess said, "I am sorry, Laine. But I needed to do something for my mom. And I wanted to do it before I left. I didn't think it would take so long. But I should have done it after I got back."

"We need to hurry. Maybe I can still get there on time," Laine said.

But she didn't think she could.

Laine and Tess hurried. But they

didn't get to the school until after 8:10.

Laine was late.

Laine saw Griff. He was on the bus. He was sitting next to a window. Steve was sitting next to him.

Laine and Tess got on the bus. Laine had to sit with Tess. She didn't get to sit with Griff.

It was a long ride to the other school. Laine was glad when they got there.

Griff got off the bus. Then Laine and Tess got off the bus.

Laine walked over to Griff.

She asked, "Why didn't you save me a seat?"

"It's your fault. You were late. You said you would be here by 8:10. But you weren't here. So I didn't save you a seat. You should have been here on time," Griff said.

Laine said, "It wasn't my fault. Tess

made me late. She wasn't ready when I got to her house. I had to wait for her."

"So? You should have planned to be at her house sooner. Then Tess would have been ready sooner. And you can't be mad at me. You didn't get here by 8:10," Griff said.

Griff was right. Laine had said she would be there by 8:10. So she couldn't be mad at him. But she wanted to be mad at him.

And she couldn't be mad at Tess either. Tess had wanted to be places on time before. But Laine had made Tess late. And Laine had always said it didn't matter. She had also said it was OK to be a few minutes late.

Laine had always thought it was OK to be late. But that was when she made others or herself late. It wasn't the same when someone else made her late.

Now she knew how others felt when she made them late.

It does matter. She should have known that before. But she didn't know it until now.

Griff asked, "Are you mad?"

"No," Laine said.

Griff said, "Good. Then we need to find some good seats. The game starts soon."

Laine didn't get to ride with Griff on the bus. But she would sit with him at the game.

And she would now try to get to places on time.

GET JAMMED!

Tristan Howard

A
LITTLE **APPLE**
PAPERBACK

SCHOLASTIC INC.
New York   Toronto   London   Auckland   Sydney

*To Babs and Amy,
from D. W. and M. P.*

ISBN 0-590-96221-3

Copyright © 1997 by Daniel Weiss Associates, Inc. Conceived by Edward Monagle, Michael Pollack, and Daniel Weiss. Grateful acknowledgment to Stephen Currie. All rights reserved. Published by Scholastic Inc. LITTLE APPLE PAPERBACKS and the LITTLE APPLE PAPERBACKS logo are trademarks of Scholastic Inc. Cover art copyright © 1997 by Daniel Weiss Associates, Inc. Interior illustrations by Marcy Ramsey.

Produced by Daniel Weiss Associates, Inc.
33 West 17th Street, New York, NY 10011

12 11 10 9 8 7 6 5 4 3 2 1   6 7 8 9/9 0 1/0

Printed in the U.S.A.   40

First Scholastic printing, February 1997

Chapter 1

"Two points!" Julie Zimmer shouted. She threw the basketball into the air. It soared toward the net.

"No way!" Matt Carter scoffed.

I moved forward. If Julie's shot went in, the red team—my team—would have two points. But if it didn't, then someone would have to get the rebound.

Whack! The ball hit the rim and dropped into my arms. "Pass it, Catherine!" Joanna Wrightman yelled.

Matt jumped toward me. His blue jersey was way too big for him. "Nanny nanny boo-boo!" he shouted. "Catherine's it, Catherine's it, she's a stupid idiot!" He made a face at me.

"Shoot!" Julie called.

I was just about to let go of the ball when someone shouted, "Catherine! Freeze!"

Oh, no! It was Mitchell Rubin. He was pointing straight at me. His fingers were crossed, and mine weren't.

"Rats!" I said. I stopped moving.

Mitchell and I have a freeze bet. We tell each other to freeze every chance we get. To keep from being frozen, you have to have your fingers crossed when the other person says to freeze. But my fingers weren't crossed.

How could they be? My basketball team was playing a practice game. And

how can you shoot with your fingers crossed?

I'm Catherine Antler. Our team's real name is the Rangers, but everyone calls us the Leftovers. We're the players no one wanted. It's kinda easy to see why: Julie only cares about how she looks; Josh Ramos carries his blankie in his pocket; and Danny West gets so interested in being a sports announcer, he forgets he's playing the game.

"Mitchell!" I said. Once you're frozen, you have to stay that way until the person who froze you says "Defrost!"

I waited for Mitchell to say I could defrost. But he didn't.

My nose itched.

"Catherine!" Brenda Bailey shouted. "Throw the ball!"

"I can't!" I yelled. "Mitchell has to defrost me first!"

"Catherine's frozen! Catherine's frozen!" Mitchell chanted. His fingers were still crossed. "Brrr! I bet you're cold."

"Pass!" Julie shouted. Her jersey looked like a big red stoplight.

Suddenly Matt grabbed the ball out of my hands. He moved so fast I saw only a flash of blue. "Hey!" I yelled.

"You weren't using it," Matt yelled back. He dribbled down the court and shot the ball into the net.

"Two points for the blues!" Matt gave a thumbs-up sign.

Lucy Marcus took the ball and threw it toward me. "Catherine!" she shouted.

I wished I could lean over and pick

up the ball. But I couldn't. Mitchell still hadn't defrosted me.

"Grab it, Catherine!" my mom shouted. She's our coach.

"Mitchell!" I yelled. "Defrost me right this minute!" I was getting angry. I always defrost people right away.

"I don't think so," Mitchell said. He pretended to shiver inside his blue jersey. "Don't you like being a block of ice?"

And then I realized something. Mitchell wasn't ever going to defrost me! His uniform was blue. He was on the other team!

No wonder he was being so mean.

"Mitchell!" I cried. "Please!" I tried to look very sad.

The ball bounced closer. Mitchell picked it up again. He passed it down the court. And the blue team scored again.

I was still frozen.

"Mitchell!" I snapped. My legs were aching. My hand hurt from sticking out so long. "Let me go, or else!"

Mitchell grinned. "Or else what?" he asked.

I tried to think of the worst thing I could. "Or else I'll freeze you at school when we go to the cafeteria. And you'll miss lunch." Mitchell is very skinny. He really needs his lunch!

"It won't work," Mitchell said. "I always cross my fingers."

"Then I'll pull your fingers apart," I threatened. My nose was *really* itching now. I wanted to scratch it so badly.

Mitchell shook his head. "That's cheating. I'll just keep you here forever. You make a nice statue."

A statue? Uh-oh. This was getting serious. I tried to think the itch away, but

it just made the itching worse. I wished I could drop a brick on Mitchell.

"I'll *never* defrost you," Mitchell said, his grin even bigger.

"You said 'defrost'!" I yelled. "I'm free!" I wiggled my whole body. Everything seemed to be working all right.

"I didn't mean that kind of defrost," Mitchell protested. But I ignored him and ran down the court after the ball.

I made sure to cross my fingers first.

"Pass!" Brenda shouted.

I could see Brenda near the other basket. But I wasn't sure I could throw the basketball that far.

Especially not with my fingers crossed!

It was the next day, and we were playing the Dodgers. The score was tied, 8–8. Basketball's pretty easy to understand. If you throw the ball into the basket, you get two points.

There is one tricky part, though. You can't run with the ball. To move the ball, you can pass it. Or you can run while you bounce it—that's called dribbling.

"Catherine!" Brenda yelled.

My fingers hurt from being crossed for so long. But I didn't dare uncross them. I took a deep breath.

"Catherine Antler has the ball!" Danny said in his announcer voice. "What will she do? Stay tuned."

Brenda was too far away, I decided. So I passed to Alex Slavik. Alex dribbled it—right off his foot.

Did I mention that Alex's feet are as big as boats? Well, they are.

"You should have passed to me!" Brenda shouted. She ran toward us just as one of the Dodgers got the ball and started to dribble.

"Get it, Brenda!" my mom shouted.

"Get it, Bwenda!" Lucy's little sister, Ava, jumped up and down on the sidelines. There was a big grin on her face. "Get it, Bwenda!" Ava's voice is pretty loud for such a little kid.

But as Brenda reached for the ball, I heard another voice. An even louder voice.

FREEZE!

"Freeze, Brenda!"

It was Matt. He was sitting on the bench, pointing at Brenda. His fingers were crossed.

Brenda skidded to a stop and froze solid.

"Fweeze!" Ava shouted joyfully. She crossed her own pudgy fingers. "Fweeze!"

"Matt!" Lucy yelled. "Defrost her!"

"We lost her?" Matt giggled. "Did you say we lost her?"

"Matt!" Brenda groaned. But the Dodgers had scored. They were ahead, 10–8.

And Brenda was still frozen in the middle of the court.

"It's all your fault, Matt Carter!" Lucy stamped her foot. "I'm never going to speak to you again."

"Okay," Matt grumbled. He said the magic word: "Defrost!"

"That's better," Brenda said. She ran off.

I grabbed the ball. "Lucy!" I yelled. I threw it right to where Lucy was standing.

Only she wasn't looking. Instead she was pointing to the bench. She had *lots*

of fingers crossed. She looked like a crab.

"Freeze, Matt!" she said. Her eyes danced.

"Too bad!" Matt sang out. He held up his hand. His fingers were still crossed.

"Lucy!" I yelled. The ball was whizzing toward her head!

Lucy turned toward me. "You can't freeze *me*, Catherine," she said—just before the ball hit her in the head, right above the ear!

"Ow!" Lucy yelled. She fell to the floor and grabbed her head. "I think I'm dying!"

"Lucy okay?" Ava asked worriedly. "Ava do it herself. Ava get basket." She pointed to the net.

"Don't even think about it," I said with a shudder. I could just see Ava trying to shoot a basket.

Mom ran out onto the court. Matt

was close behind. "You're okay," he said when he reached Lucy.

"Really?" Lucy asked. "My brains didn't fall out?"

"You just need to put some ice on your head," Mom said comfortingly.

Ice. The word made me think of something.

But Matt beat me to it.

"Freeze, Lucy!" he cried out. And he pointed his crossed fingers right at her.

"Matt!" Lucy said angrily. "Just because I uncrossed my fingers to feel my head, that doesn't mean you have to freeze me!"

"You didn't *have* to uncross your fingers," Josh pointed out. "You could have done it like this." He pushed his long hair out of his eyes. His fingers were crossed.

"Or you could have crossed your ankles," Julie suggested.

14

Joanna nodded. "Or your eyes." She made her own eyes cross. She's pretty good at it.

Mom sighed. "Come on, Lucy," she said.

"I can't, Mrs. Antler," Lucy answered. "Matt froze me."

Mom scratched her head. "Matt and Lucy, could we stop this silly game, please?"

Stop the game? We all stared at Mom.

Adam Fingerhut cleared his throat. "You can't just stop playing freeze, Mrs. Antler," he explained.

"Yeah," Brenda added. "The whole point is to get other people when they're not looking."

Mom sighed. "Then please defrost Lucy, Matt."

Matt made a face. "Okay. You can defrost."

"Thanks, Matt." Lucy got up with a groan. But before she rubbed her head, she made sure to cross her fingers.

"Freeze is a neat game," Danny said as Lucy went off with Mom. "Who wants to make a freeze bet with me?"

That was easy.

We all did!

Chapter

When the second half of the game started, I got the ball and passed to Matt. Matt passed to Brenda. Brenda passed to Adam. Things were going great.

"Shoot, Adam!" Mom yelled.

Adam dribbled three times. "Out of my way!" he shouted. He jumped and

threw the ball toward the basket.

Only it never got there. The ball arched up and came right back down. One of the Dodgers grabbed it.

Adam wiggled his hand. "It's hard to shoot with your fingers crossed," he sighed.

"Fweeze!" Ava piped up from the bench. But we ignored her. After all, she didn't have a freeze bet with any of us.

"De-fense! De-fense!" chanted the Rangers on the bench.

When you have the ball, you're playing offense. When you don't, you're playing defense. I ran to guard the girl with the ball. I spread my arms out so she couldn't dribble past me.

"De-fense! De-fense!" I thought I heard Mitchell calling from the bench.

Wait a minute, I thought. I looked at

the bench. Mitchell was actually yelling something different.

"De-frost! De-frost!" he was shouting. There was a huge grin on his face.

I rolled my eyes. But when I looked back at the girl with the ball, my heart sank. While I'd been watching Mitchell, she had dribbled right by me—and was shooting the ball into the net!

"Catherine!" shouted Mom. "Pay attention!"

"Yeah, pay attention," Matt told me.

I blushed. It was Mitchell's fault for making me look away.

Matt dribbled down the floor. "Air Matt!" he shouted. He shot, and the ball dropped through the basket.

"Great shot!" Brenda patted his shoulder.

"That was as high as the *trees,* Matt!" Joanna shouted from the bench.

Matt stopped moving. He glared at Joanna.

"Come on, Matt!" I called. The Dodgers had the ball, and they were running hard. Without Matt, we would have only four people to guard them. They would score for sure.

But Matt still didn't move. He was balancing with one leg in the air. I frowned. He looked frozen.

I scratched my head. Who had frozen Matt?

"Joanna!" Matt bellowed. "Defrost me!"

The Dodgers' bench cheered. Oops! I'd been so busy watching Matt, I hadn't noticed that they'd scored.

"Me?" Joanna looked confused. "I didn't freeze you!"

"You did so!" Matt insisted. "Defrost me this instant!"

I thought back. Joanna had said, *That was as high as the* trees, *Matt!*

And suddenly I knew what had happened.

"Matt!" I yelled. "Joanna never froze you at all. She said *trees,* not *freeze*!"

Matt frowned. "She did?"

"Yeah!" I said. With my hands I made picture of a tree. "She said 'as high as the *trees.*'"

"Freeze, Catherine!" Lucy shouted.

Oh, no. I couldn't believe it!

I'd uncrossed my fingers to draw the tree in the air. And Lucy had noticed.

Matt had never been frozen. Not really.

But I sure was!

Chapter

Thump, thump, thump.

That was the sound of basketballs on the floor.

Thump, thump— "Oops!"

I sighed. I could also hear the sound of basketballs rolling away.

We were at practice the next day. We'd lost to the Dodgers, 20–12. So we were working on getting better.

But it wasn't easy.

All of us had our fingers crossed.

And it's hard to dribble when your fingers are crossed!

"Do it like this," Brenda suggested. She bounced the ball with one hand and crossed her fingers with the other. "There!" she said proudly. "Nobody can freeze me!"

I tried it, too. "Hey, yeah!" *Thump, thump, thump.* "It works!"

Tweet! The whistle blew. "Switch hands!" Mom called.

Switch hands? I bounced the ball with one hand. Quickly I crossed the fingers of the hand I had just used and uncrossed the fingers of the other. Then I bounced the ball with my other hand.

It was tough, but I did it.

"Freeze, Catherine!" Yin Wong said.

"You can't get me," I told her. I turned to show her my fingers.

23

Big mistake. The ball bounced up and hit me in the jaw.

Tweet! "Now bounce it back and forth," Mom told us. "First dribble with one hand, then the other. Alex, Yin, and Lucy—go!"

Back and forth? Uh-oh.

"Like this?" Alex asked. He slammed the ball down on the floor. Then he tried to figure which fingers to uncross.

Too late. The ball hit him on the knee.

"Ow," Alex said. He bent over to rub his leg.

I sighed. Alex is really good at science. You'd think that someone who's really good at science would know which fingers to cross, wouldn't you?

"I can dribble with my elbow," Lucy said. She bent her arm. All her fingers

24

were crossed again. She tried to bounce the ball with her elbow, but she missed.

"Strike one!" Danny said.

Mitchell poked me in the ribs. "I dare you to uncross your fingers," he whispered.

"No way," I whispered back. "You'd freeze me."

"No, I wouldn't," Mitchell said. "Promise."

My fingers hurt from being crossed so long. Maybe if I just uncrossed them for one teeny second . . .

I slid my fingers apart and relaxed them.

"Freeze!" Mitchell shouted.

"You're mean!" I said. "You promised!"

"I lied," Mitchell said with a grin. "Now you're frozen."

"But—" I began. Then I noticed

something. Of course! "I'm not frozen," I told him. "My ankles are crossed."

I pointed to my ankles. Good thing I'd crossed them when I sat down!

"Darn," Mitchell said. He snapped his fingers. Or at least he tried to. All his fingers were crossed.

"Matt, Danny, and Brenda," Mom called. "Go!"

Matt did pretty well. He dribbled back and forth, and he always knew which fingers to cross and which ones to uncross.

Danny and Brenda had a harder time. Danny kept blowing bubbles with his wad of gum. He always does that when he's nervous. And Brenda kept losing her ball. Finally she crossed her knees. She looked pretty uncomfortable.

But at least she had both hands free.

"Don't fall, Brenda!" Mitchell said.

He uncrossed his fingers and leaned forward to watch.

I started to tell Mitchell to freeze. But Joanna beat me to it. "Freeze!" she said.

"No way!" Mitchell said. "My toes are crossed."

"Toes don't count," Joanna said.

"Toes do too count," Mitchell argued.

"No, they don't." Adam shook his head. "You can't cross your toes, anyway. They don't stretch far enough."

"They do so!" Mitchell tugged off his shoe.

"Your feet smell," Julie commented.

"Uh-uh!" Mitchell yanked his sock off and wiggled his toes. "I washed them last week."

We watched him pull his big toe over his second toe. It sort of looked

crossed, but it didn't stretch all the way across.

"Ha!" Joanna said. "See, you can't do it."

"Not like that," Mitchell said quickly. This time he pulled his second toe over his big toe. Sort of. "Like *this*."

Adam rolled his eyes. "I can cross my toes better than that. Watch!" He started to pull off his shoe.

"I bet *girls* can do it," Julie said. "Girls have nicer toes than boys do."

"Yeah," I agreed. I took off my shoes and socks. "See?"

I lifted my foot into the air. Then I tried to fold my big toe over my second toe. I pulled harder and harder, and—

Tweet!

Mom was standing right there. And she didn't look very happy.

"Mitchell, Catherine, and Adam,"

she said. "Didn't you hear me calling? It's your turn."

We stood up quickly. But we left our shoes and socks where they were.

Let me give you some advice: *Never* dribble a basketball barefoot.

Because it really stings when a basketball hits your toes!

Chapter 5

"I don't understand this freezing game," Mom said to me a few days later. We were on our way to the game against the Cardinals.

"It's called *freeze*," I explained. "Not *freezing*."

"Whatever," Mom said. "Don't your fingers get tired of being crossed all the time?"

"They aren't crossed all the time," I said. "I don't cross them at night. Or when I'm with just you."

I didn't want to admit it, but Mom was right. My fingers *did* get tired of being crossed.

Mom grinned. "Freeze!" she said.

I made a face. "Mom, you can't freeze me. We don't have a freeze bet."

"Aren't there any time-outs in freeze?" Mom asked.

I shook my head. "You can freeze people any old time. That's what makes the game fun."

When we got to the gym, I watched the Cardinals practice. They didn't look good. Some of their players were as bad as Alex.

"Go, Wangers!" Ava shouted.

GO RANGERS!!

I grinned at her. "Slap me five, Ava!" I told her.

Ava slapped me five. "What happened to your hand?" she asked with a frown. "All bended." She pointed to my crossed fingers.

"It's okay, Ava," I said. I uncrossed my fingers to show her they still worked. But I crossed the fingers on my other hand, just in case. "It's all part of playing freeze."

"Fweeze," Ava repeated. She tried to cross her fingers.

"Hey, Catherine!" Mitchell called. "Watch me cross my ears!" He pulled on his ears and waved them back and forth.

"My hair is always crossed," Joanna pointed out. She flipped her braids. "You can't freeze me!"

"Oh, that doesn't count," Adam said. I laughed. Adam has a crew cut. He doesn't have enough hair to cross!

"I'm crossing my arms today," Lucy said. She folded her arms across her chest. "Crossing your fingers all the time is too hard."

"How will you dribble?" I asked her.

Lucy shrugged. "With my elbows."

"Fweeze!" said Ava. But we ignored her.

When the game started, I was on the court with Alex, Yin, Julie, and Matt.

We were bigger than the Cardinals.

We looked stronger than the Cardinals.

Of course, one thing worried me a little.

None of the Cardinals had their fingers crossed.

The referee threw the ball into the air. Julie jumped as high as she could and tapped it to Matt.

"Yay, Matt!" Joanna shouted. She was careful not to say a word that rhymed with *freeze*.

Matt dribbled toward the Cardinals' basket. He kept one hand on the ball while the fingers on his other hand stayed crossed. First he dribbled around one Cardinal. Then he dribbled around another.

"Go, Matt!" Brenda yelled. She pumped her fist in the air.

"Two points!" Matt sang out. He picked up the ball with both hands and let it fly.

I'd seen him make that shot a hundred times. Maybe a thousand! But that day the ball didn't come close to the basket.

"Off the rim!" Mitchell chanted.
Matt stared down at his hands.

I frowned. I wondered if he was having trouble because his fingers were crossed.

I went back on defense. I was guarding a short kid. One of the other Cardinals passed the ball to him. But it was close enough for me to reach. "I've got it!" I yelled.

"Antler with the steal!" Danny announced.

I lunged forward. I touched the ball. But with my fingers crossed, I couldn't grab hold!

The ball bounced away. The Cardinals got it back.

"Butterfingers!" Julie complained.

I glared at her. "Oh, yeah?" I snapped. "*You* try catching the ball with your fingers crossed."

The Cardinals shot. The ball bounced off the backboard. "I've got it!" Julie

shouted. She leaned over to grab the ball—

But it hit her palm and rolled away across the floor.

The Cardinals got the ball *again*.

"Julie!" I was angry. "You should have had that one!"

"Well, I tried," Julie said.

"Fweeze!" Ava cried out. She was still trying to get her fingers to cross. I glared over at her. Ava was beginning to get on my nerves.

I guess Lucy thought so, too. "Be quiet, Ava," she said.

The kid I was guarding took a shot. I tried to block it, but I couldn't reach high enough. The ball went into the net.

2–0, Cardinals.

Alex got the ball and began to dribble. But halfway down the court, he tried to change hands. First he looked

at his fingers. Then he looked back at the ball. By the time he figured out which fingers to cross, it was too late.

The Cardinals had stolen the ball.

"Alex!" I wailed.

Alex's shoulders slumped. "I'm sorry," he said. "I just didn't want to get frozen."

The short kid shot the ball from a long way out. *Swish!*

I groaned. I wished somebody would freeze Alex. Julie, too.

"Let's freeze everybody!" Matt said. "Except me. I'll beat these guys five on one!"

I thought about saying that I was pretty good, too.

But I didn't.

I had a feeling Matt wouldn't agree. And I didn't want to be frozen.

So I decided I would keep my fingers crossed—forever!

Or at least until the game was over.

Chapter 6

We had cookies at halftime. It was hard eating them with our fingers crossed. But it was better than being frozen.

$$\frac{1}{2} \text{Time}$$

"What kind of disease do you children have?" Mom asked.

"Disease?" Alex patted his red hair

with his crossed fingers. "I don't have any diseases, Mrs. Antler. I went to the doctor on Tuesday, so I know."

"Say *ah*," Mitchell told me.

I opened my mouth and stuck out my tongue. "Hmm," Mitchell said. He looked into my throat. "I can see your toenails."

"Can not," I said.

"What disease?" Julie wanted to know. She looked worried. "If I throw up, my uniform will get all gross."

"Not a stomach disease, Julie," Mom said. "I think this disease is called *crookedfingeritis*."

"Crooked-finger-itis?" Lucy frowned. Then she grinned. "Oh! This isn't a disease, Mrs. Antler. We're playing a game." She uncrossed her fingers. "See? It's called—"

"Freeze!" Yin said. She pointed her crossed fingers at Lucy.

"Don't interrupt, Yin," Lucy said. Her ponytail swung from side to side.

"I didn't interrupt," Yin said. She was smiling. "I told you to freeze!"

Lucy stared at Yin. Then she looked at her fingers. "Oops," she said—and sat very still.

"Lucy fweezed," Ava said loudly.

"Well, it seems like a disease to me," Mom said. "What game are you here to play?"

Mitchell raised his hand. "Freeze," he said.

Mom shook her head. "Anyone else?"

"Basketball," Julie said. "But playing freeze is more fun."

Mom sighed. "Does anyone know what the score is?" she asked.

We looked at each other—all of us except for Lucy, that is. She was still frozen, so she couldn't move her head.

"Um . . . twelve to eight?" Alex guessed.

"Sixteen to two," Mom corrected him. "Who's ahead?"

"The Cardinals," Brenda said. "I think."

"But that doesn't matter." Danny stuck out his hand. He had put a rubber band on his hand so that his fingers wouldn't uncross. "If I keep crossing my fingers, no one can freeze me," he said.

"But you won't score any baskets, either," Mom said.

Danny nodded. "That's okay. What's *really* important is not getting frozen."

The referee blew the whistle to start the second half.

"Defrost," Yin told Lucy.

I went onto the court and jumped for the ball. But I couldn't reach it. One of the Cardinals got it instead.

"Stop him, Josh!" Mom yelled.

Josh jumped forward. His arms were folded in front of him. I thought he would grab the ball with his hands, but instead he reached out with his elbow.

"Use your hands!" Mom shouted.

"I can't!" Josh shouted back. "I'm crossing my arms!"

Of course, I thought. That made sense. His fingers were probably tired. If he crossed his arms, he couldn't be frozen.

The Cardinal with the ball dribbled toward Brenda. "Get the ball, Brenda!" Mom shouted.

Brenda hopped forward. She was twisted like a pretzel. One leg was

wrapped around the other. She reached for the ball, but she crashed to the ground instead.

"Brenda!" Josh moaned.

"I'm crossing my ankles," Brenda explained. She tried to get up. But it was hard with her legs wrapped together.

"Catherine!" Mom was shouting. "Grab the ball!"

"Ball!" Ava screamed. She was having more fun than anyone.

The ball! I dashed for the basket— just in time to see the Cardinal with the ball toss it into the net.

"Oh, well," I sighed. My fingers were really aching by now. I wished I

had a rubber band. Or something else I could cross, like my teeth or my stomach. Maybe I could cross my heart and hope to die, I thought.

I passed to Adam and uncrossed my fingers for just a second.

"Freeze, Catherine!"

Mitchell had noticed.

I stood as still as a statue and watched Adam. He had both hands stretched out in front of him, like a zombie. And he was dribbling with both hands at once.

"Adam!" Mom cried.

The ball bounced off the floor. Adam hit the ball again. It slammed back to the ground, way in front of him.

"What are you doing?" Brenda asked.

Adam ran forward to the ball. But this time he hit it so hard he couldn't catch up. The Cardinals grabbed it.

Adam showed us his hands.

"My fingers were getting too tired," he said. "So I decided to cross my thumbs!"

Chapter

7

"What's in the box, Mrs. Antler?" Alex asked the next day. We were about to play the Dodgers again.

Brenda smacked her lips. "I hope it's cookies."

"Cookies!" Ava shrieked. "Yummy, yummy!" Then she pointed at Mom and said, "Fweeze!"

The Cardinals had beaten us the day before, 34–2! But Mom was looking pretty happy. I wondered why.

I also wondered if I could uncross my fingers without anyone noticing. It wasn't much fun to keep them crossed. But it was even less fun to be frozen.

"Is it new uniforms?" Julie asked hopefully. "Maybe this time the color will match my hair."

Mom pulled off the lid. We all crowded around to see what was in the box. Inside were about fifty long strips of cloth.

"Bandages?" Yin exclaimed.

"We don't get hurt *that* much," Adam said. "Not even Alex gets hurt that much."

Mom grinned. "These aren't in case someone gets hurt," she explained. "They're to help you play better."

"Play better?" Danny looked puzzled. "How can we play basketball better with bandages on?"

"Basketball?" Mom looked surprised. "Who said anything about basketball? I got you these so you can play freezing better."

"You mean freeze," Matt said.

"Oh, darn," Joanna said. "I *just* uncrossed my fingers. They were so tired! I was hoping no one would notice." She froze.

Matt looked embarrassed. "Defrost," he said.

"Thank you," Joanna said. Then she crossed her fingers, but she made a face while she did it.

"I got the idea from Danny and his rubber band," Mom said. "Who has tired fingers?"

We all raised our hands—with our fingers crossed.

"See?" Mom said. "I know you love to play freeze during basketball games.

The bandages will help keep your fingers crossed. Catherine, come here and cross your fingers, please."

I stood up and crossed my fingers, two by two. Two pairs on my right hand, two pairs on my left. Everything but my thumbs.

"Perfect!" Mom said. She wrapped each pair of fingers very tightly inside a bandage. When she was finished, I couldn't wiggle my fingers at all.

"Now you can't possibly be frozen," Mom said. She smiled. "Well, aren't you going to thank me?"

"Um—thanks, Mom," I said. I sat back down.

"You look like a mummy," Adam told me.

"Danny?" Mom held up four new bandages. "Your turn."

"Me too?" Ava looked up at my mom. "Ava have some, too?"

Mom smiled. "Sure, honey. You can have some bandages, too," she said as she started wrapping Danny's hands.

When the game started, the boy who played center for the Dodgers frowned at me. "What's with your hands?" he asked.

"Oh, nothing," I said. "All of us have bandages. See?" I pointed at the rest of the Rangers.

He looked even more confused. "How come?"

"To help us play our game better," I explained.

"You're crazy," he said.

Well, maybe I was crazy—but I wasn't frozen!

The referee tossed the ball up between us. I jumped higher than the other kid,

but when I touched the ball, I couldn't tap it where I wanted it to go. My bandages were in the way. The ball fell to the floor, and the Dodgers grabbed it.

"De-fense!" Yin chanted.

"E-fense!" Ava held up her hands, which were wrapped in bandages. They looked like lion paws, only white.

The Dodgers passed the ball down the court. One of their players took a shot. The ball clanged off the rim and into Josh's arms.

"Josh!" Julie called from the other end of the court. "Pass!"

Julie was all alone. If Josh could get the ball to her, she would score for sure.

Josh reached his arm back, getting ready to pass. He can throw a basketball farther than anybody. He only uses one hand. But this time the ball rolled off his fingers and hit the ground.

"Josh!" Julie called again. She cupped her hands around her mouth—sort of. It was hard with her fingers all bandaged.

"I'm trying!" Josh picked up the ball with both hands. He held it awkwardly between his palms.

"Hurry!" Julie shouted.

Josh put both his hands over his head and let the ball fly. But it bounced three times before it got near

Julie, and a Dodger picked it up first.

I ran toward the kid who had picked it up. She was dribbling toward the basket. I stretched my arms out and touched the ball—

But my fingers wouldn't close! They were so stiff, I could only hit the ball. I couldn't grab it. And I knocked it right back to the Dodger player.

She grinned at me. "Thanks!" she said. Then she dribbled around me and shot—right into the basket.

Dodgers 2, Rangers 0.

Brenda went to get the ball and throw it in.

"Good try, Catherine," Mom said. "Too bad about the ball. But at least you didn't get frozen, right?"

Chapter 8

Brenda rolled the ball to Danny. She couldn't even pick it up with her big bandaged hands. Danny caught it between his knees.

"West dribbles up the floor!" he announced. But the ball squirted away from him. "West's bandages are too tight!" Danny added. "He loses the ball."

The ball bounced toward me. I leaned down to pick it up. But it bounced right off my fingers.

"Now Antler loses the ball, too!" Danny called.

"Ball gone?" Ava asked from the bench.

I hadn't known it was so hard to do things with your fingers all wrapped up. How did mummies manage?

"I got it!" Julie cried. She sprinted toward the ball.

"And Zimmer has it!" Danny announced. "She—wait a minute, folks. . . ."

I watched the ball roll off Julie's fingers, too.

"Now *Zimmer* drops it!" Danny said. "The Leftovers are turning into the Butterfingers! You heard it here first."

The Dodgers grabbed the ball.

My fingers were really hurting now. Every one of them wanted to wiggle. I was glad no one could freeze me. But I

was beginning to realize there was a problem.

With *all* of us wrapped up, I couldn't freeze anybody.

And what was the use of playing freeze if everyone was safe all the time?

The Dodgers shot again. Josh tried to block it. But the shot went over his arms and into the basket. 4–0.

"Two points!" Danny said in a gloomy voice. He blew a bubble with his gum. It popped all over his face. He tried to pull the gum off, but he couldn't. Not with his hands wrapped up like that!

"This is silly," Lucy said. "I wanna do a cartwheel." She started to do a cartwheel.

"Lucy! Don't!" I yelled.

Too late! Lucy crashed to the ground. She had forgotten something

very important: You need your fingers for cartwheels!

"Ow!" she yelled.

"Are you all right?" Mom asked.

"I guess so." Lucy stood up slowly.

"Ava help," Lucy's little sister piped up. She stuck out her bandaged hands. "Ava do it herself!"

I sighed.

The way things were going, she probably *could* play basketball better than any of us!

Matt came into the game to replace Lucy. "Give me the ball!" he shouted. "I'm the star!"

Brenda shoveled the ball over to Matt. He dribbled. The ball went way in front of him each time he bounced it. But he always caught up. And in a few seconds he was standing next to the Dodgers' basket!

"Shoot!" Brenda called.

Matt held the ball between his palms. He made a face. "How do I throw it when I'm all wrapped up like this?" he asked.

"Quick!" Alex shouted. "The Dodgers are coming!"

Matt tossed the ball—underhand. It sailed over the backboard and hit the wall. "Darn!" he said.

"Dodgers' ball!" called the referee.

"Ava want ball!" came a voice from behind us. I turned around to see where Ava was—and my heart sank.

Ava was halfway up the pole that held our basket!

I couldn't imagine how she had climbed up that far with her big mummy fingers, but she had. She wrapped her legs around the pole and lifted one hand. "Gimme ball!" she yelled. "Ava get basket!"

"Ava!" Lucy cried, horrified. "Hold on!"

I ran forward as fast as I could. What if Ava fell? I could imagine it happening. With her hands all bandaged, maybe she couldn't grasp the pole. "I'm coming!"

"No want *Caffrin*!" Ava's voice was angry. "Want *ball*!"

I skidded to a stop under the basket. I gulped. Ava had climbed higher than my head. I reached up to grab her. "Come on, Ava," I said in as calm a voice as I could manage, trying not to frighten her. "I'll get you down."

But I couldn't.

My own fingers were bandaged too tightly. I couldn't get a grip on Ava's body.

I wished I'd never even *heard* of freeze. Then my fingers wouldn't be bandaged, and Ava's wouldn't be, either. I wished

we were playing better, too. Then Ava wouldn't think she had to climb up the pole to get a basket for us. I tried to grab her again, but it was no use.

"Mom!" I yelled. I needed help, and I needed it fast.

"Coming!" Mom yelled back. She started to run across the court—just as Ava let go of the pole with her other hand and began to fall.

"Ava!" Lucy screamed.

There was only one thing to do, so I did it. I leaned back and let Ava fall right onto my chest. Then I grabbed her in a bear hug. You can do that even if your fingers are bandaged.

Ava started to cry.

I could feel my heart thumping inside my chest. It sounded just like a basketball being dribbled.

I breathed a sigh of relief.

I was scared, and my chest hurt where Ava had fallen on it.

But she was safe. And *that* was the most important thing of all.

Chapter 9

"Mrs. Antler?" Julie asked at halftime. We were trying to eat pretzels with our fingers wrapped. It wasn't easy.

But it was easier than playing basketball. We were behind, 14–0. We hadn't even been able to hit the backboard. Not once.

Julie stuck out her lip. "Do we have to wear these bandages all the time?"

"Yeah," Yin chimed in. "My fingers hurt!"

"You can't do *anything* in them," Danny complained. His chin was still pink with bubble gum. "You can't get gum off your face."

"You can't do cartwheels," Lucy agreed.

"You can't play basketball," Matt said. "You can't dribble or pass or shoot."

"And you can't—" Alex began. He stopped and looked at Ava, who had taken off her bandages and was eating a pretzel.

But I knew what he had been going to say: *You can't help Ava if you're wearing bandages.*

"So do we *have* to wear them?" Julie asked again.

Mom stroked her chin. "I thought you kids only cared about freezing each other."

"But that's no fun anymore!" I burst out. "Everybody always has their fingers crossed, so they can't be frozen. And playing freeze is dangerous when little kids are around. Can we take the bandages off?"

"Please?" Josh begged.

"Are you sure?" Mom asked, looking at all of us. "What if your fingers get too tired? You'd have to uncross them, and then you'd be frozen."

"No, we wouldn't," Matt said. "My fingers need a break. I think we should quit playing freeze until the game is over."

Mom looked surprised. "I thought you couldn't have time-outs in freeze."

"You aren't supposed to," Danny explained. "But maybe we should right now. For a little while."

"Okay." Mom shrugged. "You kids are in charge. Who wants to

stop freezing until the game is over?"

Twelve hands shot into the air.

"Fine." Mom pulled out a pair of scissors. In a minute my fingers were free. It felt so good to wiggle them again!

Matt, Josh, Alex, Brenda, and I went in to begin the second half. The referee tossed the ball up.

This time I was able to tap it to Josh, who started dribbling and took off toward the basket. And the ball didn't bounce away from him. When he was close enough, he grabbed it and threw it into the net.

"Two points!" Danny said into his pretend microphone.

I slapped Alex five. It was better than slapping mummy fingers!

The Dodgers dribbled back down the court, but Matt stole the ball. "Rangers on a roll!" he shouted. He started to dribble—*really* dribble. And he shot the regular way, too, not underhand.

"Carter makes the bucket," Danny announced. "It's Dodgers fourteen, Leftovers four."

"Go, Wangers!" Ava yelled.

We scored some more baskets, but

time began to run out. With two minutes left, we were losing by six points.

I sat next to Mitchell on the bench. "It's nice not to have to cross your fingers, isn't it?" I said.

Mitchell grinned. "I didn't agree to the time-out," he said.

"Yes, you did," I said. "We all did."

"Not me," said Mitchell proudly. "I had my fingers crossed, remember? And if you have your fingers crossed, you can lie." He held up his fingers. They were still crossed.

My eyes got very big. "Don't you dare!" I said.

"Maybe I will and maybe I won't," Mitchell said.

On the court, Brenda passed the ball to Adam.

"I could freeze Adam right now," Mitchell boasted.

"You'd better not!" I threatened him.

Adam jumped. He timed his shot perfectly. Two points! I cheered and clapped. Clapping is another thing you can do better without bandages.

The Dodgers' center passed the ball toward our basket. But Yin leaped forward. She grabbed the ball with the tips of her fingers—and hung on! I jumped up. "Go, Yin!" I shouted.

Yin dribbled around two Dodgers. She threw the ball as high as she could. *Swish!* It landed right in the net.

"All right!" I yelled.

"I should have frozen her," Mitchell

told me. "She would have looked silly hanging in the air."

I leaned forward. We were losing by only two points now. We could even win!

If Mitchell didn't start freezing people.

One of the Dodgers dribbled down the court. He turned this way and that. But whichever way he turned, there was Matt.

"Go, Matt!" I yelled.

Matt reached forward and knocked the ball out of the Dodger's hands. It rolled down the court—and right to Julie. She leaned over and grabbed it. Then she straightened up and shot.

I held my breath.

The ball hit the backboard. Then it bounced off the rim. Up. Down. Up. Down—and into the net!

Tie game!

"See?" I told Mitchell. "If Matt's and Julie's fingers had been crossed, we wouldn't have scored."

"Let's go, Rangers!" Mom shouted. Adam and Joanna started to chant: "Rangers rule! Rangers rule!"

Let's Go Rangers!!

"I could say you-know-what," Mitchell threatened.

"If you do, I'll—" I stopped. Lucy had just caught a pass that was supposed to go to one of the Dodgers!

"Go, Lucy!" we all yelled. Alex stamped his big feet.

Lucy dribbled, but she looked scared. There was a line of Dodgers in front of her. "Help!" she shouted. "Somebody help me!"

"Here!" Matt ran behind her. "Pass!"
Lucy gave him the ball.

PASS IT!

"Here I come!" Matt shouted.

There were three Dodgers in the way. "He'll never make it," I said out loud. Not even Matt could get around three of them.

But Matt surprised me. First he looked as though he was going to go to the right. Then suddenly he switched hands and went to the left. He was past one Dodger!

Then Matt switched hands again— and dribbled around the next player!

"Go!" we shouted.

Matt faked left and drove right,

around the last Dodger player. Now no one was between him and the basket.

"Shoot, Matt!" Julie cried.

Matt dribbled once more. There were three seconds to go.

Just then I noticed Mitchell out of the corner of my eye. His crossed fingers were pointing right at Matt!

I grabbed Mitchell and held his mouth closed tight. With my other hand I pried his fingers apart.

"Mmm—mmm—mmm!" He couldn't talk with my hand over his mouth.

Matt jumped higher than I had ever seen him jump. He drilled the shot toward the basket.

The ball hung in the air for a moment. Then it sliced down through the net.

Two points!

"And the Rangers win!" Danny

shouted. He threw his hands into the air. "All *right*!"

Matt came off the court, grinning. "I told you I could score if I didn't have those bandages on," he said.

"I knew you guys could do it," Mom said proudly.

"What's our treat, Mrs. Antler?" Brenda asked.

"Frozen yogurt," Mom told her.

"Fwozen!" Ava repeated. She tried to cross her fingers. Then she made a face and uncrossed them quickly. "Fwozen, yucky!"

Matt wiggled his fingers. "There's just one thing I'd like to say now that the game's over."

"What's that?" I asked.

Matt grinned, and like lightning, his fingers were suddenly crossed.

"Freeze!" he said.

THE LEFTOVERS

by Tristan Howard

Don't be left out!

The Leftovers are the wackiest team in any league.
No matter what the sport, fun and laughs are always
part of the game plan.

BASEBALL:

❏ BBS56923-6 **The Leftovers #1: Strike Out!** $2.99
❏ BBS56924-4 **The Leftovers #2: Catch Flies!** $2.99

SOCCER:

❏ BBS89896-5 **The Leftovers #3: Use Their Heads!** $2.99
❏ BBS92133-9 **The Leftovers #4: Reach Their Goal!** $2.99

BASKETBALL:

❏ BBS96219-1 **The Leftovers #5: Fast Break!** $3.50
❏ BBS96221-3 **The Leftovers #6: Get Jammed!** $3.50

Available wherever you buy books or use this order form.

Send orders to:
Scholastic Inc., P.O. Box 7502, 2931 East McCarty Street, Jefferson City, MO 65102

Please send me the books I have checked above. I am enclosing $_____ (please add $2.00 to cover shipping and handling). Send check or money order—no cash or C.O.D.s please.

Name_____Birthdate_____

Address_____

City_____State_____Zip_____

Please allow four to six weeks for delivery. Offer good in U.S. only. Sorry mail orders are not available to residents of Canada. Prices subject to change.

LO796

**Amber Brown doesn't want much—
just a little credit for trying!**

AMBER BROWN
WANTS EXTRA CREDIT
BY PAULA DANZIGER

Amber is in deep trouble.
Her room is a mess, her
homework is late, and to
top it all off, her mom is
dating someone!
No matter what Amber
does, it isn't enough! Why
won't anyone give Amber
credit for trying?

**Coming in March to
bookstores everywhere**

Don't miss Amber's other adventures:
AMBER BROWN IS NOT A CRAYON
YOUR CAN'T EAT YOUR CHICKEN POX, AMBER BROWN
AMBER BROWN GOES FOURTH

AMB79●